Fort...
Adventures in the Liaden Universe® Number 28
Sharon Lee and Steve Miller

COPYRIGHT PAGE

Fortune's Favors: Adventures in the Liaden Universe® Number 28

Pinbeam Books: www.pinbeambooks.com

"Fortune's Favors" and "Surebleak: Dudley Avenue and Farley Lane" are original to this chapbook

Cover Design: SelfPubBookCovers.com/RLSather
ISBN: 978-1-948465-04-5

DEDICATION

To Michael J. Walsh and Ian Randal Strock
publishers and booksellers
who help make the
science-fictional world
go 'round

FORTUNE'S FAVORS

ONE

It was to the gayn'Urlez Hell in lower Low Port that his feet finally brought him, over the objections of most of himself.

There were those who dismissed Low Port as a miserable pit of vicious humanity where lived predators and prey; the roles subject to reversal without notice.

Those contended that there was nothing of value in Low Port; that it was worth the life of any honorable person to even attempt to walk such streets.

They. . .were not wrong, those who lived in the comfort of Mid Port and the luxury of High; and who bothered to give Low Port half a thought down the course of a Standard Year.

They were *not* wrong.

But they lacked discrimination.

It was true that there were very many bad and dangerous streets inside the uneasy boundaries of Low Port, and then –

There were worse.

The gayn'Urlez Gaming Hell occupied the corner of two such thoroughfares, and the best that could be said of them is that they were. . .somewhat less unsafe than the Hell itself.

Mar Tyn eys'Ornstahl had made it a policy – insofar as he was able to make policy – not to enter gayn'Urlez, much less work there.

Today, his feet had trampled policy, and Mar Tyn only hoped that he would survive the experience.

So anxious was he for that outcome, in fact, that he took the extreme action of. . .arguing. . .with his feet.

On the very corner, directly across from the most dangerous Hell in Low Port, Mar Tyn – turned to the right.

His feet hesitated, then strode out promptly enough, even turning right at the next corner, with no prompting from him, toward the somewhat safer streets where he was at least known.

Another might have assumed victory, just there, but Mar Tyn had lived with his feet for many years. It thus came as no surprise when they failed to take his direction at the next corner, bearing left, rather than right, until they stopped once more across the street from Hell.

He sighed. That was how it was going to be, was it?

Best to get on with it, then.

#

The barkeep was a thick woman with cropped grey hair and a prosthetic eye. She gave him a glance as he approached and leaned her elbows on the bar.

"Got reg'lars on tonight," she told him, pleasant enough. "Two days down there's a bed open, if you want to reserve in advance. Reservation includes a drink tonight and a hour to study the layout. The House takes six."

Mar Tyn smiled at her over the bar.

"I'm not a pleasure-worker," he said, gently.

She frowned.

"What *are* you, then?"

"A Luck."

She might have laughed at him; he expected it. She might equally have accepted him at his word; most did. Who, after all, would claim to be a Luck, if they were not?

He did not expect her to be *angry* with him.

"A Luck! Are you brain-dead? Do you know what happened to the last Luck who worked here?"

He did not. Not actually. Not *specifically*. He could guess, though.

"Her winner beat her, and robbed her of her share?"

The barkeep looked dire.

"Her winner followed her home, beat her, raped her, murdered her, took the money, her child – and for good measure, fired the building."

She paused, and took a breath, ducking her head.

"They say she was lucky to the last – no one died in the fire."

Mar Tyn took a breath.

"Ahteya," he said.

That earned him another hard glare, the prosthetic eye glowing red.

"You knew her?"

"No. We – Lucks – we know. . .*of* each other, in a general way. I had heard that a Luck named Ahteya had been killed –" Rare enough; most who hired a Luck didn't care to court the *ill*-luck that must come with such an act, though Lucks were still regularly beaten and robbed. Mar Tyn supposed that it was a matter of necessity. Violence was Low Port's primary answer to hunger and want, and it could be reasoned that a Luck whose gift did not protect them was *meant* to be robbed.

"I hadn't heard where she'd been working," he told the barkeep. "Or that she had a child."

"Well, now you know, and I hope the knowledge improves your day. You can leave."

"No," he said, with real regret – for her, and for him. "I can't."

Another red glare.

"*Can't*?"

"Despite appearances, I'm not a fool. When I saw where I had come to, I tried to walk away. With what success you see."

He produced an ironic bow.

"I believe the choice before us is – will you allow me to sign the book, or will I freelance?"

The color drained out of her face.

"You poach here and gayn'Urlez will break all of your bones. Slowly."

"I understand," he told her.

She sighed, then, hard and defeated.

"You're *certain*?" she asked.

"Rarely have I been more certain," he said, and added, for the wounded look in her natural eye. "I don't like it, either."

She reached beneath the bar.

"Here's the book, then; sign in. House's piece from your cut is twelve."

He glanced up from the page, pen in hand – "Not six?"

"Six is for whores; they comfort the losers, and convince them to try again, which is good for the House. If a Luck's good, they're bad for the House, 'cause their winner's going to go big."

"I'm good," he told her, which was neither a lie nor a boast. "The Lucky Cut is – ?"

"Thirty-six."

"*Thirty-six?*"

Great gods, no wonder Ahteya's winner had wanted her share. Even after she had paid the House its twelve percent. . .

"House rules," the barkeep told him. "gayn'Urlez wants them to think before they hire. Better for the House, if they don't hire."

"Of course."

He signed, and sighed, and pushed the book back to her. She glanced at his name.

"All right, Mar Tyn. The House pays for your winner's drinks. You get a meal before you start work, and as much cold tea as you can stomach. I'll show you the back way out, too."

That last was truly kind. He wondered how well she had known Ahteya.

"Thank you."

"Stay alive, that's how you thank me," she snapped, glancing over his head at the clock.

"Let's get you to the kitchen for your supper. It's near time for the earlies to get in."

#

His supper long eaten, and his third cup of cold tea sitting, untouched, by his hand, Mar Tyn sat behind the small red table, within good view of both the door and the bar. His winner had not yet arrived, and he might have been inclined to wonder why his feet had brought him here, were it not for the certainty that he would find out soon enough.

He had, very occasionally, been delivered to this place or that, only to find that. . .something – perhaps the simple act of obeying the compulsion of his gift – had altered circumstances sufficiently that he was no longer required in that particular place and time. On every one of those occasions, however, he had felt. . .a release. His feet lost their wisdom halfway down a busy thoroughfare, or his sudden thought that it would be pleasant to have a cold treat resulted in his arrival at the ice vendor's stall.

This evening he felt no such release, and a trial thought – that it would be pleasant to go back to his room in the attic of Bendi's House of Joy – did not result in his standing up from behind the table, approaching the bar, and informing the 'keeper that he was quit.

Mar Tyn sighed.

No, his winner was taking her time, that was all. His gift *did* prefer to be beforetime in these matters. His part was to recruit his patience, and be vigilant.

He looked at his cup of tea, then around about him. There was something that was said on the streets – that *like called to like*, and here in gayn'Urlez Hell one could see ample evidence of that small truth.

Those who framed the residents of Low Port as brutes and less would need only to look through gayn'Urlez' door to be vindicated. Gambling was the primary draw – and those it drew ranged from the desperate, willing to do anything for a meal, to those who had the means to oblige them. Opposite his corner was another table, like his, clearly visible from both door and bar. The woman sitting there was the current local power to contend with. Her name was Lady voz'Laathi, and she held six entire blocks under her protection, with gayn'Urlez Hell being the center-point. Two bullies stood behind her, guns and knives on display, and those who dared approach the table did so with hunched shoulders and bowed heads.

As if she had felt his glance, the lady turned her head and met his eyes. For a moment, they regarded each other. The lady spoke over her shoulder and one of her two protectors stepped away from the table, and crossed the room.

Mar Tyn drew a deep breath. Surely, he thought, *surely* not. . .

"Luck," the man said, standing on the far side of the red table.

"Gun," he answered, politely.

"My lady asks you to look aside. She's got no need of your gift."

Mar Tyn bowed his head, pointedly averting his eyes.

"My regards to your lady. Please assure her that I am here on other business."

"I'll tell her that. She says, too, that you're on her ticket. Eat, drink, whatever you want. My lady's no enemy of luck."

"I honor her," Mar Tyn said, not entirely without truth. There were those who would have had an audacious Luck shot for his incautious glances. "The House feeds me this evening."

"I'll tell her that, too," said the lady's Gun, and turned away, but not before he had dropped a coin to the tabletop.

Mar Tyn's reactions were Low Port quick. His hand flashed out, covering the bright thing while it was still spinning and pinning it flat to the table.

He glanced quickly around the room, careful to avoid the lady's eyes, though he could feel her attention on him. He pulled the coin to him, and slipped it away into a pocket. It was a valuable thing, and a dangerous one, and he wished it had not been given.

Well, but given it had been; and, once accepted, it couldn't be returned, unless he wished to risk offering the lady an insult that would certainly be Balanced with his life.

He took a breath.

That he had been given no chance to refuse the favor. . .

. . .that. . .was disturbing.

Mar Tyn closed his eyes, drew a deep breath, held it for the count of twelve – and exhaled.

There was no tremor from his gift; nor sizzle of anticipation in his blood.

He opened his eyes, and turned his head to make a study of the room behind the bar.

Try, he told himself, considering the greater room, and the crowd at the card table. . .*Try not to be a fool.*

The Luck's Table was set as far as possible from the games of chance. That was prudent; proximity *was* a factor in the working of his gift. He personally felt that he was not situated quite far *enough* from the games to avoid influence, if his gift was feeling playful – which, fortunately, it was not.

He did not, of course, say this to Sera gayn'Urlez when she came to his table, shortly after the Gun had left him.

"You're the Luck Vali signed in, are you?"

"Yes, Sera. Mar Tyn eys'Ornstahl, Sera."

"Why choose to come here?"

"Sera, forgive me; I did not *choose* to come here."

That earned him a grin, unexpected and attractive on a broad face with one short white scar high on each cheek.

"So, you've been here before?"

"Twice, Sera. Once, when I was a child, with my mentor. Again, when I was newly my own master."

"Not since?"

"No, Sera."

"Why not? Didn't earn enough?"

"Sera, I earned well that night. My winner was killed by a wolf-pack, three paces from the door, and I swore that I would not help someone to their death again."

The frown was as fearsome as the grin had been attractive.

"I don't allow wolf-packs on my corner, or on either street, for the length of the block."

Mar Tyn had heard about this policy, which was enforced by the lady at whom he had been bidden not to stare. Such enforcement benefited both, after all, and gayn'Urlez *did* sit at the center of the lady's base.

"Sera's brother was gayn'Urlez," he said. "When last I worked here."

Interest showed in her face.

"My brother died six years ago. You're older than you look."

In fact, he did look younger than his years, and had in addition come unusually young into the fullness of his gift. Which gayn'Urlez had no need to know.

He therefore inclined his head, acknowledging her observation.

"Vali told you the rules and the rates?"

"Yes, Sera."

"Questions?"

"I collect my commission, less the House's fee, from the floor boss?"

"That is correct. Your winner will also collect, minus the House's fee, from the floor boss." She paused, seeming to consider him.

"If you feel that you're in danger from your winner, or from anyone else on the floor, you have Vali send for me, understood?"

This was an unexpected courtesy. Mar Tyn inclined his head.

"Yes, Sera."

"Yes," she repeated, and sighed. "I'm in earnest, Luck eys'Orn-stahl. Vali would have told you about Ahteya. I don't necessarily want Lucks operating out of my premises, but that doesn't mean I want them beat and killed for doing what they were hired to do."

"Thank you for your care," he said, since it seemed she expected a reply, and it was good policy to be polite to the host.

She stood another moment or two, studying him. He gave her all his face, feeling no twinge from his gift. His was to sit there, then, and wait, until waiting was over.

\#

The room had filled and the play had grown raucous before Mar Tyn felt a shiver along a particular set of nerves, and looked up to see a man approaching the Luck's Table. He wore a leather jacket of a certain style, though to Mar Tyn's eye he was no pilot. His face, like so many faces in Low Port, bore a scar – his just under the right eye, star-shaped, as if someone had thrust a broken bottle, edges first, at him.

"Luck for hire?" he demanded, voice rough, tone irritable.

"Ser, yes," Mar Tyn said.

"Stand lively, then! I've work for you tonight!"

Mar Tyn rose, looking over his prospective winner's shoulder to Vali at the bar. He caught her prosthetic eye, and she inclined her head, teeth indenting her lower lip.

"Gods, you're nothing but a kid! Do you think this is a joke?"

"No, Ser," Mar Tyn said truthfully. "I'm not so young as I seem."

"You can influence the *kazino*, can you?"

Well, no, not exactly, but there was no coherent way to explain how his gift operated to someone who did not also bear the gift. And this man did not want an explanation – not really. He wanted a guarantee that Mar Tyn would make him a big winner, which, Mar Tyn realized, considering the warmth of his blood, he would very likely do. Barring stupidity, of course. Not even Luck trumped stupidity.

So.

"Ser, the *kazino* is a specialty," he said, which was almost true. Wheels, machines, and devices were the easiest touch for his Luck. Cards were more difficult, and Sticks the most difficult of all. His win average for Sticks was fifty-eight percent, only a little over what native probability might achieve; while his success rate with the machines was very nearly seventy-three percent. Keplyr had found his affinity for *kazino* amazing. But Keplyr's gift had favored cards.

"All right, here."

The man grabbed his shoulder and pulled him to a stop by the *kazino* table.

"Get busy," he said, and leaned close, voice low and full of threat. "If I catch you slacking off, I'll break your fingers. You don't need your fingers to give me a win, do you?"

"No, Ser," Mar Tyn said quietly. "But pain will disturb my concentration."

"Then keep your mind on the job," snarled his soon-to-be winner. He reached into his jacket pocket and withdrew two quarter-cantra, which he gave to the croupier in exchange for a small handful of chips.

Mar Tyn closed his eyes, the better to see what his gift might tell him.

"Well?"

He answered without opening his eyes.

"Everything on red three."

#

His winner had done well, though he did not seem pleased with either his success or Mar Tyn's obvious diligence on his behalf. He did not win all of the spins, of course; chance simply did not operate that way. However, he won very nearly three-quarters; and his losses were – save one – minor.

The big loss – Mar Tyn had felt it looming, and directed that a prudent bet be set on green eight. It wouldn't have done to cash out of the table entirely; not with the rolling waves of plenty he sensed hovering just beyond the loss. Besides, it put heart in the other players to see that even a man augmented by Luck was not immune to a set-back, and he owed at least that much courtesy to the House.

So, he had directed that prudent placement, but his winner – his winner had not been drinking. Perhaps he was drunk with success; certainly he was arrogant.

In any case, he turned his head, met Mar Tyn's eye, and placed twice the requested amount on the square.

It could have been worse; at least the man had not let everything ride on the spin. Also, the loss had the happy outcome of demonstrating that Mar Tyn knew his business far better than the man who had engaged him.

After that, his winner placed his bets as directed by his Luck, though he did so with ill-grace, and continued to win. The table lost players, and filled again, in the way of such things, until – two hours before the day-port bell forced even gayn'Urlez to close – the man abruptly swept all his winnings off the table, and carried them to the floor boss' station.

It was gayn'Urlez herself at the desk, which ought not have surprised him, Mar Tyn thought. She tallied the chips, did the conversion to coin, and counted out the whole amount.

That done, she paused, the money on full display until the winner stirred and growled, "Agreed."

"Excellent," she said. "We will now pay your just debts. Thirty-six percent to the Luck."

She counted it onto the desk before him, fingers firm.

"Agreed," said Mar Tyn in his turn; "and twelve percent to the House."

She smiled faintly.

"Indeed."

The appropriate amount was subtracted. He accepted the remainder and slid it away into various pockets.

"You are done here for this night, Master Luck," gayn'Baurlez said then. "The House can bear no more."

"Sera, yes. My thanks."

She did not even look at him, her fingers already busy with the remaining money.

"You will of course share a drink with me," she said to the winner. "On the House."

Mar Tyn was already through the bar's pass-through, on his way to the back exit, but he heard the winner clearly.

"No."

#

He ran, his feet and the rest of himself of one accord.

Fleetness was a survival skill in Low Port, and Mar Tyn had thus far survived. Still, his winner, though heavier, had longer legs, and a great motivator in the money in Mar Tyn's pocket. If it came to an outright race, the larger man would overtake the smaller.

Happily, the race was not nearly so straightforward.

Mar Tyn's goal was not his attic room at Bendi's. No, he was flying full-speed toward one of his bolt-holes, a cellar window left off the hook beneath a pawn shop in Litik Street. He was a bare two blocks from that slightly moldy point of safety, confident that he could reach it handily.

In fact, he had the pawn shop in view, and was veering to the left, aiming for the alley that unlatched window opened into. . .

When his feet betrayed him again.

He hurtled past the pawn shop, even as he flung out a hand to snatch the post at the corner of the building, intending to swing himself 'round and into the alley.

"Hey!" he heard a man shout behind him. "You! Luck! Stop!"

Dammit.

Mar Tyn took a hard breath – and let his feet take him.

#

His winner caught him at the corner of Skench and Taemon, when a speeding and overburdened lorry lurched into the inter-section as he started through. He missed his stride, staggered, threw himself to the right – and was lifted from his feet by a grip on his collar.

His winner tossed him, casually, into the wall of the building on the corner. Luckily, the wall was plas, not stone, and Mar Tyn bounced, ducking out of the way of his winner's fist.

The second punch connected, knocking him back into the wall. Mar Tyn used the slight give, and kicked out, hard and ac-curate. His winner yelled, doubled over – and Mar Tyn was gone, hurtling across the intersection, guided by feet or fear, it hardly mattered. He had no taste for being beaten, nor did he care to buy out of a beating by surrendering the evening's earnings. He had a far better use for –

His feet dashed down an alleyway, a dark tunnel with a light at the end.

A courtyard, he saw, and the gate standing, luckily, open. Much good it would do him. A dead-end was still a dead-end, and his winner would have him.

He saw it, as his feet threw him into the yard – a window, there on the second floor, showed a light.

He might get lucky, after all.

"The house, the house!" he shouted, as his feet sped him for-ward. "Thieves and brigands! Be aware!"

The grip this time was on his shoulder, and the wall he con-nected with was stone.

The light flared and fragmented; he twisted to the left, dodging the next blow, hearing his winner curse as his fist struck the wall, and the grip on his shoulder loosen.

He tore free, intending to run back through the gate, but his own feet tripped him, and he went down to the cobbles on one knee. His winner spun, face shadowed, light running like quicksilver along the edge of the blade as he raised it.

Mar Tyn took a breath and shouted.

"The house! Murder!"

. . .and dove to the cobbles between his winner's feet, rolling, knocking him off-balance.

He heard the metal cry out as the knife struck stone, its brilliance swallowed in the shadows, and lurched to his feet, turning this time toward the house, where more lights had come on. He heard shouting – and his collar was gripped.

He was thrown against the wall again, and held there as his winner slapped him hard, driving his head against the stone.

All the lights went out; he felt his jacket torn open, a hand exploring the pockets, heard a grunt of satisfaction, and release of the punishing grip that held him upright.

He slid to the cobbles, the light coming back, smeared and uncertain.

The first kick broke his arm, and he screamed, earning a second kick, in the ribs.

A distant noise broke on his befuddled ears, and a woman's voice, speaking with authority.

"Who is brawling in my yard? Her Nin bey'Pasra, you rogue! Have I not told you often enough to stay away from here?"

A shadow loomed in the smeary light, snatching his winner and spinning him about as if he were nothing more than a child's toy made from twisted rags.

A blow landed; his winner staggered, and it occurred to Mar Tyn that this was his final chance to live out the night.

Run, he told himself, but he had no strength to rise.

Instead, he lay there on the cobbles while a large red-haired woman, briskly efficient, dealt with Her Nin bey'Pasra, slapping him into the wall as an afterthought, stripping him of his jacket as he slumped; at last picking him up by scruff and seat, frog-marching him to the gate, and pitching him into the alley.

Metal clashed – perhaps, Mar Tyn thought muzzily, she had thrown him into the garbage cans.

The woman turned, grabbed the gate and pulled it to, leaning down as if to get a closer look at the latch.

Perhaps she swore; her voice was low, the words nonsensical. She pulled a piece of chain from somewhere in the shadows, and wrapped the latch, muttering the while.

Then she crossed the yard, and squatted next to Mar Tyn. He blinked up at her, the light making a conflagration of her hair.

"Can you rise?" she asked him.

"I believe so," he said, and found that, with her arm, he could, though he crashed to his knees when she withdrew that kind support.

"My head," he muttered, raising his good hand, only to have it caught and held in firm fingers.

"I see it," she said, and raised her voice, "Fireyn!"

He flinched.

"There is nothing to fear here," she told him, her large voice now soothing and soft. "You were lucky that our gate was open."

"And why was that?" came another voice, this one male.

"The latch was broken again," the woman answered him. "We are in need of a solution there."

"Tomorrow," said the man, kneeling beside her and looking into Mar Tyn's face.

"You may put yourself in our care," he said with a gentleness rarely given even to children. "You have come to the safest place in Low Port."

He smiled, wry in the smeary light.

"I understand that is not so very much to say, but, for now, at least, you are safe. My name is Don Eyr; this lady who succored you is Serana. Fireyn, who is coming to us now, is our medic. May we know your name?"

"Mar Tyn eys'Ornstahl," he managed, as the medic approached him down a long tunnel edged with fire. He wanted only to close his eyes, and surrender to that the kindly dark, but he owed them one more thing. They must be told of their peril.

"I am. . ." his breath was coming in short, painful gasps, but he forced the words out. "I am. . .luck. . ."

The darkness reached out. He embraced it, sobbing. The last thing he heard before he was taken utterly was the man's voice, murmuring.

"Indeed, you are that."

Interludes

Mar Tyn woke to a multitude of aches, and opened his eyes upon a thin, fierce face. Two achingly straight scars traced a diagonal path down her right cheek, white against tan skin.

"Medic?" he whispered. There had been a medic – or at least, a medic on the way. He recalled that, particularly, for a medic in Low Port was a wonder of herself.

His observer dipped her chin in approval, and added, "Fireyn. Tell me your name."

"Mar Tyn eys'Ornstahl."

Another dip of the chin.

"Your right arm is broken; your ribs are accounted for. You have proven that your head is harder than our wall, so you need not make that experiment again. I used a first aid kit on the ribs, the head, and the arm, and injected you with an accelerant, which will speed healing. The arm is your worst remaining problem. You will need to wear a sling, even after your other wounds allow you to leave your bed."

He licked his lips.

"How long –" he began, but the darkness rushed up again, swallowing the thin, clever face, amid all of his sluggard thoughts.

#

He woke feeling tired, and opened his eyes to a different face, not quite so thin, nor yet so fierce, with a clear golden complexion rarely found in Low Port. The features were regular; cheeks un-scarred; eyes brown, and serious.

"Do you know me?" he asked. His Liaden bore an accent – tantalizingly unfamiliar.

"You are Don Eyr," Mar Tyn answered. "I recall your voice."

Don Eyr smiled.

"It was rather dark, wasn't it? You may be pleased to learn that Fireyn wishes you to rise, and walk, and afterward make a report of yourself. She will also be observing you with her instruments."

He tipped his head, and Mar Tyn followed the gesture, finding the medic standing at a tripod across the room.

The room – it was small, but very light. He turned his head, finding a window in the end wall; a clean window, through which the afternoon sun entered, brilliance intact.

"When?" Mar Tyn asked.

"Now," Fireyn said. "If you are able. If you are not able, then I will be informed."

He marked her accent this time, and noted the way she stood, balanced and alert. One of the Betrayed, then, which made sense, of her paleness, and the precision of the cuts that had formed her scars.

"What she means to say is that, if you are not able, she will immediately intensify your treatment," Don Eyr said, rising from the chair next to Mar Tyn's bed. "She was military, and believes in quick healing."

"A necessity, on a battlefield," Fireyn said.

And also on Low Port, thought Mar Tyn, putting the coverlet back with one hand. His right arm was in a sling, and he was wearing a knee-length robe.

Carefully, he put his feet over the side of the bed, situated them firmly – and rose.

He paused, but his head was quite steady; his balance secure. Looking up, he saw Don Eyr leaning against a wall, perhaps a dozen paces from the side of the bed.

Mar Tyn walked toward him, steps firm and unhurried.

Reaching Don Eyr, Mar Tyn bowed. Finding his balance still stable, he turned and walked to the window, where he paused to look out.

Below him was the yard his feet had carried him to in his race against his winner. It was a tidy space, seen in decent daylight. He particularly noted the tiered shelving, filled with potted plants.

"I hope I brought no harm to your garden," he said, turning to face Don Eyr.

"Not a leaf was bent," the other man assured him.

"Good."

He walked back to Fireyn.

"I report myself able. Shall I go?"

He heard Don Eyr shift against the wall – but Fireyn was shaking her head.

"I fear you are guilty of under-reporting," she said, and glanced over his head.

"I recommend an additional round of therapy," she said, to Don Eyr, Mar Tyn understood.

"You are the medic," came the answer. "Friend Mar Tyn."

He turned.

"This choice is yours. I stipulate that the therapy is not without risk. I also stipulate that none of those under my keeping – or, indeed, myself – have taken harm from it. If you wish my recommendation, it is that you allow it. This house will stand for your safety, while you are vulnerable. If you do not care to risk so much, that is, of course, your decision. It is understood that you may have business elsewhere."

It was gently said, and Mar Tyn was somewhat astonished to find that he believed that he was safe in this house, in the care of Fireyn and Don Eyr. Which left only the question. . .

Do I, Mar Tyn inquired with interest of himself, *have business elsewhere*?

There came no restless fizzing in his blood. His feet were as rooted to the floor. He was, he realized, at peace, which was very nearly as dangerous as believing himself to be safe.

And yet. . .his feet had brought him here; his feet were content that he remain here.

He was curious to learn why.

He turned to Fireyn.

"Additional therapy," he said. "I accept."

TWO

He woke feeling hale and bright, and more well than he'd been in his life. Opening his eyes, he discovered himself alone. The chair beside the bed had a shirt – not his – draped carefully over the back, and a pair of pants – likewise not his – folded neatly on the seat. The boots on the floor by the chair were, indeed, his, though someone had cleaned them, and even produced the beginning of a shine.

Mar Tyn sighed. His blood was effervescent, and his feet were itching to move.

Apparently, he had business to tend to, and he'd best be about it quickly.

#

He had managed the shirt, the pants, the socks – even with the sling – but the boots had proved beyond him.

Sock-foot, then, he danced lightly out of the room, along a short hall and down a metal staircase. At the bottom, he turned right, down a longer hallway, and found himself in a kitchen, warm, bright, and smelling of baking.

There was a large table along the right-hand side of the room, much be-floured, and holding a large bowl, well-swathed in toweling. Across the room, a light glowed red above what he took to be an oven, set into the heavy stone wall.

Despite the evidence of previous industry, the kitchen was at this moment empty.

Mar Tyn spied a teapot on a counter, holding court with a dozen mismatched cups. His feet assumed; he poured, bearing the brightly flowered cup with him to the window overlooking the courtyard, and got himself onto one of the two high stools there.

He waited, sipping tea; his feet at rest; his blood a-sizzle.

Footsteps in the hall heralded the arrival of Don Eyr, who bent his head, cordial and unsurprised, before crossing to the teapot, pouring, and returning to the window, slipping easily onto the second stool.

He said nothing, nor did Mar Tyn. Indeed, there was scarcely time enough for a companionable sip of tea before more footsteps sounded in the hall, overhasty, and desperate.

A girl burst into the kitchen, lamenting as she came.

"Oh, the bread! It will be ruined!"

She dashed to the worktable, snatching the towel from the bowl, shoulders tense – and loosening all at once, as she erupted into a flurry of purposeful action, a sharp punch down into the bowl before upending it and turning an elastic mass out onto the floured table. The bowl was set aside, as with her free hand she reached for a wide, flat blade. . .

"I wonder," Don Eyr said quietly from beside him, "what you did, just now."

Ah, thought Mar Tyn, and turned to face his host.

"Forgive my ignorance, but first I must know what happened, that went against your expectations."

Don Eyr glanced to the girl, who had divided her dough into two even portions, and was busily shaping the first with strong, sure fingers.

"The bread – the dough in the bowl, you see – it *ought* to have been ruined – *fallen*, as we have it. She left it too long at rise." He sipped his tea, and added.

"These matters are delicate, and. . .not always precise. Bread-making only pretends to be a science."

"Ah."

Mar Tyn sipped his tea, and met Don Eyr's eyes.

"I am a Luck. You say that this –" he used his chin to point at the busy worker – "is an art, and not a science. That there is some element of imprecision inherent in the event."

"Yes," said Don Eyr, "but in the case, she had left it beyond the point of recovery."

"You know your art, and I do not," Mar Tyn said gently. "I only say that, given what we have seen, there must have been some small probability that the bread would *not* be ruined, and my presence. . .gave that probability an extra weight."

Don Eyr sipped, eyes fixed on some point between the stools and the work table.

"In fact," he said eventually; "you altered the future?"

Mar Tyn sighed.

"So it is said. It's the reason we're banned from Mid and High Ports, and why the Healers and *dramliz* spit on us."

Don Eyr frowned slightly, his eyes on the baker, who had finished shaping the second loaf. She transferred the pans to the shelf by the oven door, covered them with the cloth, and wiped her hands on her apron.

Mar Tyn took a careful breath, surprised to find an ache in his side, as if one of the ribs had not entirely healed.

"I will leave," he said softly. "An escort to the gate –"

"There's no need for haste;" Don Eyr murmured. "Drink your tea."

The baker approached them; bowed.

"The loaves are shaped, Brother," she said to Don Eyr

"So I see," he answered. "Mind you do not neglect them in their rising. You cannot count on good fortune twice."

Which was, Mar Tyn thought, finishing the last of his tea, very wise of him.

The baker blushed, and murmured, and turned to clean the work table.

"I wonder," Don Eyr said, turning on his stool to face Mar Tyn, "if you will come and eat breakfast with myself and Serana." He raised one hand, fingers wide. "If you feel that you must go, I will not detain you, though I will ask for a moment to fetch those things which belong to you."

Mar Tyn paused, considering himself, and his condition.

His feet. . .were content. His stomach. . .was in need, noisily so.

He inclined his head.

"I would very much like to share a meal with you and Serana," he said.

He slid off the stool onto his quiet feet, and followed Don Eyr out of the kitchen.

\#

They ascended a short staircase to a room half-a-floor above the kitchen. A table set for three was under the open window. Mar Tyn glanced out over the courtyard, and realized that the light he had seen, the night his winner had caught him, had come exactly from this room.

He turned his attention to the larger apartment. A bureau stood against the wall next to the table, laden with dishes of biscuits, vegetables, and cheese; and a teapot, gently steaming.

Shelves lined the walls, overfull with books and tapes, and where there were not shelves, there were. . .pictures – flat-pics, hand-drawings, swirls of color. . .

Along the wall opposite the table was a screen, a double-lounge facing it. In the far corner, two more chairs sat companionably together in an angle of the shelves, a light suspended from the ceiling over both. A red-haired woman sat in one of the chairs, reading. There was a door in the wall directly behind her, almost invisible in the abundance of. . .*things.*

Mar Tyn's feet had taken him to larger rooms, and longer tables. But he had never been in so comfortable – so *welcoming* – a room. Indeed, by the standards of the rooms he most usually frequented, this cluttered chamber was. . .he groped for the word, and had only just achieved *luxurious* when the woman looked up from her book.

"Ah, here he comes, on his own two feet!" she said cordially, rising – and rising some more.

Her height was not so much of a surprise – she had cast the shadow of a giantess in the courtyard. No, what startled was her. . .fitness; this was not a woman who knew want, or who went often without her dinner. From her part in his rescue, he had assumed that she was a soldier, but he saw now that she was not. Fireyn – *there* was a soldier, from squared shoulders to flexed knees. This person – was upright, and strong, and – *proud*, thought Mar Tyn.

Just as Don Eyr was proud. And well-fed.

As the baker of breads, in the kitchen below: well-fed, strong. Embarrassed, but not abused.

"I strike him to silence," Serana noted, drily.

Mar Tyn bestirred himself and produced, having seen such things on tapes, a bow of gratitude.

"I mean no disrespect," he said. "I was overcome for a moment, recalling that I owe you my life."

"Glib," came the judgment from high up.

"But truthful," Don Eyr said, stepping to Mar Tyn's side.

"Serana, I make you known to Mar Tyn eys'Ornstahl, who is a Luck. Ser eys'Ornstahl, here is Captain Serana Benoit."

Well – a soldier after all?

Serana smiled down at him.

"My rank comes from worlds away, where I was one captain of many in the city guard. Security, not military."

Security, thought Mar Tyn, recalling her bent over the broken lock. *House* security. She would have questions for him. How not?

He took a breath and met her eyes – blue and bright. She smiled faintly.

"Come," she said, sweeping a large hand out, as if to show him the buffet and the table, "let us eat."

#

In general, Mar Tyn ate more regularly than many residents of Low Port – a benefit of his gift, which would have no use for him, if he were too weak to obey its whims.

The breakfast he was given at Don Eyr and Serana's table was beyond anything he had ever eaten; something other than mere food, so nuanced that he felt his head spin with the multiplicity of tastes and textures.

His attempt to eat sparingly was defeated by his host, who monitored his plate closely, and immediately replaced what he had eaten.

At last, though, he sat back, dizzy and replete, and looked up into Serana's gem-blue eyes.

She smiled at him, fondly, or so it seemed, and leaned back comfortably in her chair.

"Tell us," she said.

He sighed slightly, unwilling to face the inevitable results of having told them. But – he owed them no less than his life, and nothing but the truth would pay that debt.

Also – they had children in their care – he had heard their voices round the house and yard as he had eaten. Well-fed, strong, and prideful children, like the girl whose bread he had preserved. If the purpose that united this house was the protection of children – a purpose nearly unheard of, in Low Port. . .

The house needed to know about Lucks and the particular perils attending them – not only so that they might be more careful of who they let behind their protections, but to know the signs, should one of those in their care prove to be Lucky.

So, he sighed, but he told them – quietly and calmly, beginning with the day he found the woman he supposed to have been his mother lying on the floor of their basement room. He had thought her asleep, but she hadn't woken, not even when there came heavy footsteps and loud voices in the hallway.

That had been the first time his feet had moved him, away, *not* to the front of the house, where the voices were loudest, but down a back hallway, and into a pipe scarcely large enough to accommodate his small, skinny self, which, after some small time of crawling, led into a deserted, rubble-filled alleyway.

He had climbed out of the pipe, half-turned back toward the place he had just quit – but his feet took him, and he walked for many blocks, up and down streets he had never seen before, until he came to Dreyling's Tea Shop.

His feet took him into the shop, and marched him to the backmost table. He hoisted himself into one of the two chairs – and waited, for what, he could not have said. No one took any note of him. He tried, once, to wriggle out of his chair and go away, but some force he did not understand kept him where he was.

Eventually, a man with grey streaking his dark hair, wearing fine and neatly patched clothing, joined him at the table, called for tea and a plate of crackers, and when they had come, asked what was his name.

He disposed of the years with Keplyr as mentor and master with a single – "He took me in, and taught me how to survive my gift. He had lived a long time as a Luck in Low Port. It was his belief that his gift had called mine."

Keplyr's death, the stuff of nightmares that *still* woke him – he did not mention, only saying that, in time, he came to be his own master.

He spoke of the nature of his work, the particular risks found in gaming houses, and told the story of Ahteya as a caution for them, before finishing with is own misadventure, from which Captain Serana had so kindly extricated him.

"So," said that same Captain Serana, when finally he came to an end. "It seems to me that the first question we must ask is – *why.*"

Mar Tyn blinked at her.

Beside him, Don Eyr laughed softly, and rose, taking the teapot with him.

"Nothing occurs to you?" Serana prodded gently.

"Why," Mar Tyn said slowly, "so that you might save my life."

But Serana shook her head.

"You would have been safe at your first bolt-hole, but your feet bore you past," she pointed out. "Running on is what put you in danger."

Mar Tyn took a breath. He was not accustomed to questioning the motives of his gift, even after the instance was over. His chest was suddenly tight, and his breath somewhat short. . .

"Surely," Don Eyr said, returning to the table and leaning on the back of Serana's chair, "Aidlee's loaves were not worth so much."

The pressure in his chest dissolved in laughter.

"A shattered arm, and a broken head? No, I think we can agree there," he said, and looked again to Serana.

"Perhaps," he offered tentatively, "it was necessary that I alert the house that the gate was standing wide?"

Don Eyr and Serana exchanged a glance.

"Certainly," she said slowly, "it would have been no good thing, had some we can both name found us open. Yet. . ."

She looked again to Mar Tyn.

"There was no sign, after, that any had come back to complete their work, and been surprised to find the gate in force."

Mar Tyn moved his shoulders, uneasy once more.

"The fact that the gate had been relocked – the noise alone, when my winner caught me – might have changed intentions."

There was a light knock, and Don Eyr went away again, to the door. He returned with another teapot, newly steaming, and poured for all three before sitting down.

"Your *winner*. . ." Serana said, her mouth twisting with distaste. She took a sip from her cup, lips softening.

"We unfortunately know of your winner," Don Eyr said. "His name is Her Nin bey'Pasra. A very bad man. A thief, and also a murderer, many times over."

Mar Tyn nodded, unsurprised.

"I saw the jacket," he said. "There are those who take particular pleasure in damaging pilots, but they will take easier meat, if they must."

"Yes."

Serana sighed.

"I should have left him the jacket, perhaps. . ."

Don Eyr reached across the table, and put his hand over hers.

"It is done," he said, firm and quiet. "Serana. It is done."

"True," she said, and slipped her hand away, giving him a crooked smile.

She rose, then, and moved to the bureau. Opening a drawer, she removed a packet, which she brought back to the table, and placed before Mar Tyn.

"We will allow you to tell us," she said, sitting down and picking up her tea cup, "if that might be worth shattered ribs, a broken arm, and a cracked head."

The packet was sealed. Mar Tyn ran a thumbnail down the seam – and sat staring as the coins rolled and danced along the table.

Here was not only the Luck's portion from gayn'Urlez, he thought, but the winner's, as well.

"A considerable sum," Don Eyr murmured.

Mar Tyn took a breath.

A very considerable sum, as he was accustomed to count money. Was it worth a beating that had nearly killed him?

Maybe, he thought. Maybe not the money, particularly, but what the money might *buy* him?

Oh, yes.

. . .but there was. . .a problem.

He glanced down at the sling cradling his right arm.

"Where may I find Fireyn?" he asked.

"She has a short-term outside of the house," Serana said. "It is possible that we might be able to answer your question in her stead."

He nodded.

"I only wonder how much longer the arm must be restrained – and if," he added, as the next thought came to him – "if it *must be* restrained, or that is only *advisable*."

Serana laughed.

"Hear him! *Only* advisable! Fireyn would gut him where he sits."

"Perhaps not so much," Don Eyr protested, "though she would certainly avail herself of a teaching moment."

Mar Tyn considered them both, wondering if he might receive an answer, after their laughter had died.

"Ah, he glares. I ask pardon," Serana said. "I have myself made the error of inquiring of Fireyn if a certain protocol was necessary or *merely prudent*. And I will tell you that it is well I keep my hair thus short, for she would have surely snatched me bald."

"From this you learn that Fireyn's advice is immutable," Don Eyr said. "I am also able to tell you that she felt another three weeks would see you completely healed and whole."

Three weeks?

Mar Tyn looked at the coins on the table, seeing their worth in terms of his life.

"Might I. . ." he said slowly, "be given another dose of accelerant?"

Don Eyr shook his head.

"No more accelerant for you, my friend. It is not without cost, and you have had three doses." He held up a hand, first finger extended, "One, to keep you with us, for you were in a perilous condition, and more likely to die than to live."

Mar Tyn, blinked, recalling Fireyn's wry assurance that his head had proved harder than the wall.

"The skull injury?" he asked.

"The ribs," Don Eyr said. "Several had broken; at least one compromised your lungs. Fireyn immediately saw how it was, used the first aid kit, and employed the accelerant."

Mar Tyn drew a breath and bowed his head.

"I understand. The other occasions?"

"After you had wakened the first time and fainted almost immediately."

Mar Tyn eyed him.

"I held conversation with Fireyn; she told me her name, and asked for mine."

Don Eyr smiled, sadly.

"That was not the first time."

Mar Tyn took a breath.

"And the third time you surely recall, as you agreed to the dose."

"That, yes," Mar Tyn admitted, and asked. "Was I still so ill?"

"No more than you are accustomed to being, I think. Fireyn, however, took into her calculations that Her Nin bey'Pasra is still alive, and inclines toward holding a grudge."

"That was prudent of her," Mar Tyn said slowly. "I wonder – how long have I *been* in your care?"

"Two weeks."

"So long as that?" Mar Tyn murmured, hardly surprised; scarcely dismayed.

He let his eyes rest on the money again. *His money*.

Plus, the winner's share.

Knowing what he now knew, he asked himself again: was the money – the brighter future the money would assure him – *was* it worth a beating which, absent luck, and Fireyn, would have meant his death?

No, certainly not. . .except, he had *not* died, because neither luck nor Fireyn had been withheld from him.

That meant, then. . .

Well, and what *did* it mean?

"We have created more problems than we have solved," Serana remarked. "I regret that. Tell us what we might do, to ease your burden."

But Mar Tyn was thinking, now that Serana had put him on this unaccustomed path. His luck had brought him here. Why? Why *here*? Why had he been so badly damaged? Why put him in debt to these people – a debt he could never repay –

Repay.

He touched the money with just the tips of the fingers of his good hand.

The house cared for children, who were constantly at risk in Low Port. There would be those who would see the prosperity of the house and seek to steal it, and make it their own – witness the broken gate lock. To maintain such an establishment, with proper security – these things did not come cheap. That they existed at all in Low Port was. . .almost beyond belief.

He looked up.

"This," he said, meeting Serana's eyes, since he did not think he could meet Don Eyr's. Serana was the hard-headed one, he thought.

The ruthless one.

He cleared his throat.

"This," he said again. "I believe this is yours."

Serana's eyes opened wide.

"No, my friend, that it is not! We are established here in Low Port, but we strive – we strive to do better. There are children in the house, whom we have taken it up to educate, and so we must stand as an example to them."

Involuntarily, he glanced to Don Eyr, who nodded, solemnly.

"Indeed, that is your money. Very nearly you gave your life for it. Is it that have you no use for it?"

Almost, he laughed.

"I have good use for it," he said, and sighed. "But I cannot use it, with my arm thus."

"Why?" asked Don Eyr.

Mar Tyn sighed.

"In the Low Port, there are three houses – guild houses, you may call them – which offer a measure of safety to those Lucks who can afford the buy-in, and the monthly dues."

He took a breath.

"From least to greatest, they are: the House of Chance, the House of Fortune, and Prosperity."

"And you have here. . ." Serana placed her fingertips lightly against the coins, "enough to buy into Prosperity."

It was a question born of honest ignorance, and he did not laugh at her.

"The only way to join Prosperity is to be born there," he said gently, and nodded at the riches on the table. "That, however, will buy me a place in the House of Fortune, and pay my dues for a year or two."

Serana frowned, and looked beyond him, to Don Eyr. Mar Tyn waited, and presently, her eyes came back to him.

"These are princely prices, for Low Port."

"Yes. It is why most of us are freelances."

"But tell me why you cannot go inside of this hour and buy yourself safety. If it is for the need of a guard, perhaps one of us may accompany you."

"As it happens, it is for this." He rocked his arm in its sling. "I will be asked if I am accident-prone. That would make me a bad risk for the House."

"I see," Don Eyr frowned. "They must, of course, tend to their profit."

There was no answer to that, and Mar Tyn made none, merely frowning down at the table, and trying to work out the moves.

"What would you have us do?" Serana asked.

He stirred, and looked up at her.

"I have lodgings," he said. "But I cannot have such a sum with me, there, or on the streets."

"But, that is easy!" Serana said, looking over his head to meet Don Eyr's eyes. "We can hold it in the safe."

"Yes;" he agreed; "that is no trouble at all."

A safe. Who possessed such a thing? Well. Carmintine the pawnbroker would very likely hold this dragon's hoard for him, as she already held the greater balance of his money. She would, of course, charge him interest. With such a sum, that would be no small expense, and he was still left with the problem of transporting it through the streets.

No, best to leave it where it was.

"You understand," Serana said softly, "that there *are* children in the house, and they are our priority."

"Therefore your money is lucky," Don Eyr said, "for it will receive our same protection, though it is of far less value."

Mar Tyn stared at him, but he seemed to be serious.

"I will be pleased to leave my money under the protection of your house," he said slowly. "What interest will you charge?"

Serana half-laughed.

"What a place this is!" she exclaimed. "We will hold your money for love, my friend. Or, if you will have your Balance, we will hold it in payment for having brought more trouble into your life."

"After *saving* my life," Mar Tyn added, but there seemed to be no arguing with her, and he was suddenly aware of a small twitching in the soles of his feet.

"I feel that I must go," he said, looking between them; "now."

Don Eyr rose immediately.

"Allow me to help you with your boots," he said.

THREE

His feet took him home.

Which was to say, to the customer entrance of Bendi's House of Joy. He tried to bring his meager influence to bear; to force his purposeful march past the front and round to the back of the house, the delivery door, and the stairs to the attic room where he slept, which he was let to have so that his luck would shield the house.

Of course, his preference counted for nothing.

Cray was on the front door, a man big even for a Terran, and who thought more quickly with his fists than his head.

Still, they had never fallen out, nor had much to do with each other, beyond a nod, and a murmured greeting.

Today, however, Cray saw him approaching, and shifted to stand in the center of the door, muscled arms crossed over powerful chest.

"Go away," he said.

Mar Tyn stopped just out of grabbing distance.

"I need to see Bendi."

"Go away," Cray repeated, and Mar Tyn was wondering if his feet were so eager that they would try a dart around the big man, and through the door.

Possibly, he would be fast enough, even with the odd balance lent by the sling.

It was not put to the test however, for here came Bendi out of the house, to stand beside Cray, fists on her hips, and her face flushed so dark that the ragged gash along the left side of her face stood out like ivory.

"You! Find a cush job somewhere else, did you, Luck? See what's happened to *me* while you were gone! I've got three hurt, and a broken water pipe, because *you* couldn't be bothered to pay your rent! Do you think I'm letting you back in here now?"

"I –" began Mar Tyn, but Bendi had noticed the sling.

She stiffened, her fists fell to her sides.

"*Get out*," she snarled.

"Bendi –"

"Get out! Your luck's broken, hasn't it? Get away from me and mine before you bring down worse upon us!"

"I'll go," Mar Tyn said; understanding that this was not an argument he could win. "Only let me get my clothes from upstairs, and the money I had asked you to hold – "

"The money went to repair the pipe," she interrupted, "and I know better than to let broken Luck into my house. Go away, *now*, or Cray will kill you."

That, Mar Tyn thought, was possible. Bendi was beyond angry; she was terrified. Terrified that his broken luck would visit more grief on her house.

He was inclined to mourn the money he had given to bind her trust, and his other shirt – nearly new! But. . .he had money, he reminded himself. He could buy another shirt.

So, he went away; his feet walking him to the right, down the long block of fallen-in buildings, and right again, round the corner, and up the alley that ran between Bendi's house and the grab-a-bite next door. That was where the bolt-door was, and there –

there stood Jonsie, Bendi's partner and sometimes worker, holding a sack, which he held out as Mar Tyn came near.

"Your stuff," he said, even the Low Port patois bearing the accent of his native speech. "Nothing to do for the coins, I'm feared; long days them're spent."

"I'm grateful," Mar Tyn said, taking the sack. There was a slight rattle, which would be his sewing kit – all he had left of Keplyr – and the weight suggested that Jonsie had rousted out his second pair of pants, as well as his extra socks and small clothes.

"'s'all right," said Jonsie. "Jes' don't be seen, gawn out. Bad for both of us, that."

"Yes," Mar Tyn said feverently.

His feet turned him around, back to the mouth of the alley, and up the street, away from all of Bendi's doors.

#

The sack made walking. . .awkward.

Not that people carrying sacks were anything unusual in Low Port. In his particular case, however, he had only one good arm to use for defense – and it was occupied with the sack. He supposed he might simply push the thing into the arms of anyone who tried to take it, and make good his escape when they fainted in astonishment.

A small tremor of nerves disturbed him at the thought of giving away his clothes, even as a tactic for survival. He could, he reminded himself again, buy more clothes. *Better* clothes, though he always tried to promptly mend any tears, and to wash himself and his clothing, regularly. That was Keplyr's training, Keplyr having been Mid House, before he came of age a Luck, and his clan of respectable Healers cast him out into Low Port.

As it happened, no one tried for Mar Tyn's sack, and he turned into Litik Street where the pawnshop was located with something like a spring in his step –

His feet faltered – and stopped moving altogether.

There was smoke in the air, and a crowd down toward the middle of the street, where the pawnshop was located. The pawnshop, where he leased space in Carmintine's safe, for his money – his savings. His *considerable* savings, which had been very nearly enough to buy himself a place in Chance...

He walked, carefully, through the smoke that got thicker the nearer he came, until he was on the edge of the crowd staring at the burnt ruin of Carmintine's shop.

There was something going on at the front of the crowd, that he was too short to see. With a sigh, he carefully slipped into the mass of bodies, and squirmed forward.

It was slow going, and surprisingly painful, as his not-yet-healed arm in its sling bumped against solid bodies – and the solid bodies pushed back, or, at best, did not yield.

Finally, though, he made it to the front edge of the crowd, and there was Carmintine, sooty and grey from head to boot soles, and four others who were known on the streets as enforcers for hire. It would appear that Carmintine had just finished paying them to stand as guards on the gutted shop, and keep away those who might risk burnt fingers for the silver and gemstones they might find among the ash.

Such protections did not come cheap, and Carmintine had hired a good team that stayed bought, once they had accepted their money – at least until the first payment was missed.

Mar Tyn slipped back into the crowd, and, once beyond it, turned away. There was no use trying to speak to Carmintine now, with her livelihood gone to ash, and the hungry crowd pressing 'round. He would try again later, maybe, but he thought he knew what would happen, if he asked after the money the pawnbroker had been holding for him.

He paused in the street, changed his grip on the sack, and started away back up the street, when he heard his name called.

Glancing to the side, he saw Pelfit the Gossip in her rickety roost, waving urgently at him. He thought he would ignore the summons, then thought better of it, just before his feet turned him toward her.

"Yes?" he said, when he had arrived and all she did was look at his arm in its sling, and the sleeve of his jacket pinned up out of the way.

She dragged her eyes up to his face, and held out one unsteady, bony hand.

"Word on the street, Mar Tyn Luck."

Pelfit's ears were large. If not intelligent, she was at least shrewd, and more often than not her gossip was worth the price.

Mar Tyn set his sack down between his feet, reached awkwardly into a jacket pocket and pulled out the packet of bread and jam that Don Eyr had insisted he take with him.

"Fresh bread," he said, "and berry spread."

Her hand darted, and the neat packet was gone, vanished into layers of rags.

"Word on the street," she said again. "A dozen days now I've heard it. Mar Tyn's luck is broken, and he's a danger to all who know him."

Mar Tyn frowned. That sort of Word could be got out on the street easily enough, a matter of whispering into the ear of this Gossip and that one, with a protein bar slipped into a receptive hand as proof of the news. . .

"Word on the street," Pelfit said again, her hand extended.

He considered her.

"If you would tell me that Bendi's house has taken hurt, and the pawnbroker burned out, I have those Words, I thank you."

She sighed, her hand falling away.

"That's everything, then," she said slowly, and turned away from him. She did not wish him well.

Of course not. She'd already taken a risk, speaking to a man who wore his broken Luck plainly visible in a sling.

Mar Tyn took a breath, picked up his sack, and waited a heartbeat, to see if his feet would move him.

When they did not, he walked away up the street, taking care how he went, until he turned down a short dim alley, and slipped into a niche in the crumbling stone wall.

When he was satisfied that no one had followed him, he proceeded down the alley, until he came to a set of metal stairs, which he climbed until he reached a ledge of that same crumbling stone, that made the beginning of a graceful arch across the alley – and ended not quite halfway across.

He settled himself carefully in the shadow against the wall, made certain he could see the alley below in both directions, and set himself to think.

Mar Tyn Luck was a danger, to himself and all who know him.

That was a warning. A warning that Mar Tyn was being hunted, and those who knew him would do best for themselves by thrusting him away.

It was. . .interesting, in its way, that *he* had been given a warning. That sort of courtesy was reserved for the disagreements that might fall between Lady voz'Laathi and her rivals. Not merely a warning, but an invitation to choose sides in an upcoming war.

Mere Lucks did not go to war, though some were *brought* to war by those who sought to insure their victory.

No.

His blood ran cold, with nothing of his gift in it; merely his own reasoned certainty.

Ware, Mar Tyn Luck, whose friends will suffer.

The small mischiefs at Bendi's house; the greater one at the pawnshop – those had been. . .surety. Proof that whoever had put that Word out was in earnest.

Deadly earnest.

And, further. . .

He closed his eyes.

The warning was not *for him*.

It was for his friends – Bendi, Carmintine.

Don Eyr. Serana. The children.

The bakery, with its broken gate latch.

The bakery, where Her Nin bey'Pasra had lost his winnings – and his jacket of honor, too.

Someone – the likeliest being Her Nin bey'Pasra – was going to war against the bakery. He was calling for allies, who would share in the profits gained, which would include the children, so carefully kept, so proud, and so soft.

Mar Tyn's mouth dried. He thrust himself clumsily to his feet, the elbow of his slinged arm banging against the wall and sending a thrill of pain through his bones.

He waited, panting, until his vision cleared, then began to pick his way across the rubble, back to the top of the metal stairs.

He must return to the bakery, at once.

FOUR

For a wonder, his feet remained obedient to his will, walking his chosen route at a prudent pace. He therefore arrived at the bakery as he chose to do – at the front door. His decision was influenced by the certainty that Serana would have long ago managed the difficulty with the lock on the back gate, and that whoever kept the front door would have instructions on whether he was to be admitted.

What he would do, if the house would not admit him – he hadn't. . .quite. . .worked out.

But, as it happened, he need not have wasted any thought on that question.

He had barely gotten his foot on the lower step when the door sprung open and Fireyn leapt down to grab him 'round the waist, hoisting him and carrying him up the rest of the flight. A second of her kind, also bearing the scars of those who had been Betrayed, stood in the doorway, gun not quite showing; sharp eyes parsing the street.

He swung out as they reached him, clearing the way for their entrance; and swung back behind them, pulling the door closed.

Locks were engaged. Mar Tyn heard them snap and sing into place even as Fireyn set him on his feet in the hallway, and looked down at him, eyes squinted; an expression on her scarred face that he could not, precisely, read.

"Are you hurt?" she snapped.

"No. Not hurt. Is Don Eyr to house? Serana? I have news."

"They are teaching. We heard the whisper on the street. We were afraid, that you had heard it too late."

Mar Tyn sighed and sagged against the wall.

"Aidlee!" Fireyn raised her voice slightly, and there came a stirring down the hall in answer.

The girl who had not lost her breads appeared, wiping her hands on an apron. Fireyn nudged him forward.

"Ser eys'Ornstahl wants some tea, and a quiet place to sit until Don Eyr's class is over."

"Yes," said the girl, and smiled at him. "This way, Ser. You may rest in the book room. I will bring a tray."

#

The tray had held not only tea, but several fist-sized rolls which Aidlee named cheese breads. She filled his cup, asked him if he wanted anything else, and when he said that he was very well fixed, told him that he might find her in the kitchen if he went left down the hall from the doorway to the book room.

She left him then, and he sat in the chair she had shown him to, and drank his tea in small, appreciative sips. Such good tea, that pleased the nose as the cup was lifted, and the tongue as the sip was taken.

He closed his eyes and savored that small wonder, and when he had done, he put the cup back on the tray, stood up and looked around him.

Book room, he thought, and it was so – an entire room full of books. Upstairs, in the quiet room where he had shared breakfast with Serana and Don Eyr – he had thought *that* room held a wealth of books. But here. . .

It was not much larger than the upstairs room, but of more regular proportions. Several long tables marched down the center, bracketed by benches. Each table held four notepads – two at the top of the table, and two at the foot. At the wall nearest the door was a small table, supporting a computer. Light strips along the ceiling made the place bright, in the absence of windows.

Mar Tyn went to the nearest shelf and began to read the titles.

He had not made much progress before he heard the door open behind him.

He turned as Don Eyr entered, a white cap on his head, and an apron over all. His eyes looked tired, but he smiled when he saw he had Mar Tyn's attention, and came quickly to his side.

"We were worried," he said, grabbing Mar Tyn's good arm in both of his hands. "I am glad that you came back to us."

"You may not be glad, very soon. Have you heard the Word on the street?"

Don Eyr frowned.

"It is said that Mar Tyn the Luck is lucky no more, and has become a danger to his friends."

"Yes!" said Mar Tyn. "I ought not to have come back, only –"

Only, his money, enough to buy his way to Fortune, and, belatedly, the thought that, after all, his gift had not played him false.

First, though, to be certain.

"I had not thought to ask before – who is your protector?"

"Our protector?" Don Eyr shook his head. "We protect ourselves, here."

"That will not do," Mar Tyn said. "Not in this. They – Her Nin bey'Pasra, is my belief – has put out a call for allies. He has declared war on this place – on you, on Serana, and everyone you mean to keep safe here. He will see all you have built destroyed. You cannot stand against him alone. Here –"

He had realized on his way back – realized at last why his gift had guided him here that night; understood why he had been given no opportunity to refuse. . .

He reached into his pocket, and brought the thing out.

"Here!" he said again, and opened his fist to show Lady voz'Laathi's token.

Don Eyr glanced at his palm; his shoulders moved in a silent sigh even as the door worked and Serana strode into the book-room.

"What have we, a tableau?" she asked, stopping behind Don Eyr's shoulder, and glancing down at Mar Tyn's palm.

"Our Lady of Benevolence," she said, softly. "She is not so well-named, that one."

She raised her eyes and met Mar Tyn's glance.

"Are you one of hers, my friend?"

"I am not, but you ought to make haste to become so!" he said sharply.

He should have waited for Serana, he thought, wildly. Serana, who was ruthless, and practical – and who would surely grasp the weapon that he had brought to her hand. . .

"Now, why, I wonder?" she asked, still in that soft tone.

"Because Her Nin bey'Pasra calls openly for allies on the streets. He means to break the bakery, Serana, and destroy it all!"

She said nothing, merely continuing to wait politely, her eyes fixed on his face.

Mar Tyn took a breath, found he had no more words, spun and slapped the coin on the table.

"Use it," he said, harshly.

"Of a certainty, we will treat it as it deserves," Serana told him.

She reached out and gripped his shoulder. "You are concerned for us. It says much, and we love you the more for it. Tell me, what will *you* do?"

"I?" he stared, at a loss for a moment, though he had thought of that, thought it straight through. He would – he would. . .

Oh, yes.

"I will take my money, that you hold for me, and buy myself safety."

"This is intriguing," Don Eyr said. "But I beg you will rethink that plan, if only for the moment. Ail Den and Cisco have been keeping the streets under eye, and there are loiterers where usually there are none. They are not yet an army, but they would be able to visit a great deal of trouble upon a one-armed man, especially if he were slowed by the weight of so much money."

Mar Tyn looked at him bleakly.

"I cannot stay here."

"Because you will bring bad luck down on our house?"

It was said gently; without mockery. Mar Tyn drew a hard breath.

"There is no such thing as *bad luck*," he said straitly. "There is no such thing as *good luck*. There is only Luck, which is an. . .energy. A field. Some of us are focal points for the field, but make no mistake, *it* uses *us*. Lucks who attempt to force their gift die more quickly than those of us who are receptive, and hold ourselves ready to act in defense of our lives."

If we are allowed so much, he added silently, Keplyr's death flickering behind his eyelids.

"My gift sent me to gayn'Urlez' Hell; it drew Lady voz'Laathi's coin to me; and granted my winner what would be a fortune even in Mid Port. Luck led me here, to this place, to you, and those you protect, with this token of the lady's protection. To preserve you and your works. You had asked me *why here*? *This* is the answer. It would not have served so well, had I been killed, because you might not have found the token in my pocket, or known it for what it was."

He took a breath, looked from Serana's face to Don Eyr's.

"I beg you, do not cast this aside."

Serana looked at Don Eyr. Don Eyr looked at Serana.

They both looked back at Mar Tyn.

"It is a kindness," Don Eyr said gently. "I – we – accept that you offer us this from the fullness of your heart. We are grateful, for your regard, and for your courage, which brought you back, knowing your danger."

"You worry that we are soft, and easy to crack," Serana said then. "But you have not considered – perhaps you do not know! – that we have kept our place here for nearly four years. This is not the first time a mob has attempted to break us. We are not complacent, but we are, I think, not in as much danger as you believe us to be. Stay and stand with us. Will your gift allow it?"

He considered himself – feet at rest, blood a little quick, but without the sizzle of the field manifest. Truth told, he was doubtful that he *could* leave, if it came to that. . .

"My gift. . .insists upon it," he said, wryly.

FIVE

The streets fought for them.

He had not realized – had not been part of the life of the bakery long enough to. . .*see it.*

The bakery's influence did not stop at its reinforced stone walls. And it was a bigger place, of itself, than he had understood: a huge stone square, that Fireyn had told him had once been a barracks and military offices. One such office had a large window onto Crakle Street, which was now a shop, that sold bread, and other foods, which the. . .*neighbors* purchased with coin, or barter, or labor. Children who lived on those surrounding streets attended classes with the children who lived inside. Adults also came for classes, for meetings, for sparring sessions.

Serana and Cisco taught courses in self-defense. Fireyn taught strategy and first aid.

All taught a curriculum of self-esteem, and. . .ethics.

Ethics. . .

Mar Tyn had tried the word on his tongue in Don Eyr's hearing, and had been given a book tape for his trouble. He'd tucked it into his pocket, promising to read it after the current event was done.

For, despite the startling fact that its protectors were more than four adults and the children themselves, the war was going. . .not well for the bakery.

To be fair, neither were matters proceeding as quickly as Her Nin bey'Pasra and his allies doubtless wished.

Which was probably why they decided to bring fire into it.

The first thing they gave to the flames was the Gossip Roost at the corner of Toom Street. It was only made from cardboard and plas – and burned too fast to serve as a rallying point. Nor was anyone hurt, since the Gossip himself had taken shelter inside the bakery.

When news of his loss reached him, he had sighed, and sat, tight-lipped and silent, glaring at nothing in particular, until one of the older children came to him with a notepad.

"Bai Sly, help me sketch what the Roost looked like," the child said earnestly. "How big was it? Were there any drawers or cupboards?"

"That is so, when this is over, we can rebuild quickly," Cisco said to Mar Tyn, when they stopped at the kitchen for jelly-bread to have with them, in case they should become hungry during their shift as door guards.

"Rebuild," Mar Tyn repeated, as they moved to take over their post from Don Eyr and Ail Den.

"Yes."

"What if the invaders win?"

"They won't." Cisco threw him a grin. "If this plays like the other attacks, what's going to happen is they'll get bored in a couple days, when they find out we're not as easy as they thought we'd be, and start fighting among themselves."

They turned into the hallway that led to the side door post.

"Why don't they fire the street?" asked Mar Tyn.

There were signs of fire on every street in Low Port. Not all – or even most – had been set by bullies intent on smoking out their prey. But such tactics weren't unknown.

"They may try to fire the street," Don Eyr said as they reached the door. "But they will have a hard time of it."

"Why?"

"Fireyn and Dale –" Dale was the other one of the Betrayed attached to the bakery – "produced a flame retardant, and all the neighborhood helped to coat the buildings."

"Most of the buildings," said Cisco. "A couple are still vulnerable, like the Gossip Roost, but the most aren't."

He stepped forward.

"The Watch changes. Go get something to eat, and some rest."

"It has been quiet," Don Eyr said, and produced a weary smiled. "The watch changes, brothers."

He and Ail Den passed up the hall. There was a small *boom*, which was the far door closing behind them.

#

The riot arrived exactly two hours after Mar Tyn and Cisco had taken over the door.

Dozens of bullies came storming down the street, throwing stones, breaking doors, engaging with the defenders of the street. Knives and pipes were in evidence, employed by both sides. There were no guns – not yet. . .

Cisco swore, and pulled a comm from his pocket, stepping back to call Serana.

Mar Tyn stood his post, breath caught in horror. It came to him that the allies had gotten bored already and this rolling wave of destruction was Her Nin bey'Pasra's way of keeping them to his cause.

He sighed, then, relieved to be safe behind closed doors, rather than scrambling for cover inside the erupting mayhem – and swore aloud.

His feet – his feet were moving, and there were locks on the door; locks a one-armed man could not manipulate, even if he did know the codes.

He thrust his good hand out, bracing himself against the wall, but his feet kept walking, inexorable, toward the locked door.

There was a snap, and a flicker, as if Low Port's spotty power grid had achieved one of its frequent overloads.

Mar Tyn put his good hand out to grip the handle – and pulled the door open.

His feet marched him out into the riot. He pulled the door closed. Behind him, he heard Cisco yell.

#

His feet turned left, determinedly moving into the teeth of the riot. He was, Mar Tyn thought dispassionately, going to die. He was going to be torn into pieces, like Keplyr had been, trying to use his Luck – and who had known better than Keplyr that Luck was *no one's* to use! – trying to *use his Luck* to turn aside a mob raging down on a band of Mid-Porters, who had crossed the line with no purpose other than to bring food to the hungry.

He dodged a knife half-heartedly thrust at his belly, ducked away from a blow that would have knocked his head from his shoulders – all without a break in stride. In fact, he had gotten past the worst of the confusion and fighting before the expected hand closed 'round his collar and he was jerked backward, into a thin space between two houses.

"You!" Her Nin bey'Pasra shook him like a mongrel with a rat. "Where's my money?"

"I don't have it, Ser." The sound of his own voice astonished him. He sounded utterly calm and unafraid.

A hard slap across his mouth; his head hit the plas wall. He stood, head turned half-aside, waiting for the next blow.

Which did not come.

"Do you want to live, Luck?" snarled his captor.

What game was this? Mar Tyn turned his head slightly, watching the other out of the side of his eye.

"I want to live," he said flatly.

"Then earn your life from me!"

Another blow – and the world went black.

#

Pain brought him back to consciousness. He was lying in the dirt, his head throbbing, and Her Nin bey'Pasra looming above him, smiling.

Mar Tyn closed his eyes, seeing his own doom in that smile.

"Look at me! Unless you've decided you no longer want to live."

He opened his eyes and stared into the smile, which seemed to please the man.

"Give me victory in this war, Luck, and I will let you live."

A terrifying promise. Let to live, in Low Port, with all his limbs broken? Or with or a knife wound to the gut?

Still...

"I will try what I may do," he said, which was not a lie, and added, "Ser."

Teeth glinted.

"Try," his winner advised. "Try hard."

The shift of balance warned him; he rolled, but he could not avoid the boot that came against his weak arm in its sling. Lightning flared through his head, and he screamed.

Curling around his damaged arm, he heard Her Nin bey'Pasra speak again.

"Give me the delm of flour and all of his treasures, or you *will* know pain, Luck."

"Now, *try*!"

There came the sound of steps, retreating, of a door being heavily slammed into place and the song of a lock being engaged.

Mar Tyn lay in the dirt, and wondered if, after all, there was such a thing as bad luck.

#

He may have passed out again. He woke to a touch. A touch from a soft, very cold hand, against his cheek.

Carefully, he opened his eyes.

A small, exceedingly dirty, child was kneeling next to him. Her hair was a dusty snarl, bruises and cuts were clearly visible between the rents in her rags.

"Hello," he said, very softly, feeling Luck burning in his blood.

She continued to stare at him out of light eyes surrounded by black bruises.

"You are like my mother was," she said, her voice gritty and low. "I can see the colors all around you."

He took a breath, deep and careful, and slowly, without taking his eyes from hers, he uncoiled until he was flat on his back.

"Was your mother Ahteya?" he asked her softly.

She closed her eyes, and turned her face away.

Mar Tyn waited, his bones on fire.

The child turned back to him, desperation in the gaunt, scratched face.

"I can fix it," she said

"Fix what?"

"This," she said, and leaned forward, putting her two small hands against his newly-shattered arm.

Pain – no. Something far more exalted than mere pain flowed into him from the two cold points of her hands. He couldn't scream; he had no breath; and it continued, this strange, clear, not-pain; his arm was encased in it, and he imagined he could feel the broken bones grinding back into place.

Above him, the child whimpered, and he tried to tell her not to hurt herself, but he had no voice, until –

She lifted her hands away, and sat back on her heels. Tears made streaks of mud down her face. There was a sound, and she snapped around, gasping, but whatever – whoever – it was passed by their sturdy locked door.

Mar Tyn remained where he was, feeling nearly transparent, now that both pain and anti-pain had left him. Carefully, he raised his recently re-broken arm, turned it this way, that way; flexed his fingers.

Everything operated precisely as it should.

A Healer, he thought. *The child is a Healer.*

Awkwardly, he rolled into a seated position, and put two good arms around his knees. The child turned to face him again, and he saw that she was shivering.

He reached into his pocket and pulled out the packet of bread and jam, worse for its recent use, but certainly still edible.

"Eat," he said, offering it to her on the palm of his hand.

She stared at it; he saw her wavering on the edge of refusing, but one grubby hand snatched out, as if of its own accord, and she was unwrapping the treat.

"He'll be back," she whispered. "He'll beat me, unless I make the bakery unlucky. I can't make the bakery unlucky – can you?"

"No," he said softly, watching her cram the bread into her mouth. "I can't. There is no such thing as good luck or bad luck. There is only Luck."

She swallowed, somewhat stickily, and he wished he had water for her.

"He says I'm a Luck," she said. "A bad and *stupid* Luck."

"He knows nothing. What is your name?"

"Aazali."

"Aazali, my name is Mar Tyn, and I *am* a Luck, as your mother was. Thank you for healing my arm. I will take you away, and I swear to you, on my mentor's honor, that Her Nin bey'Pasra will never beat you again."

She looked up at him.

"You can promise this?"

He paused, listening to his blood.

"I can," he said, with absolute certainty. "I will take you to a safe place, to rest and to heal." That first, and most importantly. The rest of what must happen – that could wait until she was safe with Don Eyr and Serana.

"Where will you take me?" she asked him. She had stopped shivering, he saw. That was good.

"I will take you to the bakery. Will you come?"

"When the bakery falls and he finds me there, he'll kill me," she said matter-of-factly.

"The bakery is not going to fall," Mar Tyn said, certain again, as he was so rarely certain.

She considered him for a long moment.

"He killed my mother," she said.

"I know. He will not have you."

Another pause, as if she were looking very nearly at those colors she claimed to see spiraling around him.

"I'll come," she said at last.

"Good."

He rose, effortlessly, to his feet. She rose less easily, and wavered where she stood.

"It will be best," he said, "if I carry you."

Another ageless stare from those bruised light eyes.

"Yes," she said.

He bent and took her into his arms. She weighed nothing.

"Arms around my neck," he told her. "Head down. Eyes closed."

She did as he asked. Her hair scratched his chin.

He took a breath, standing quiet; and felt his feet begin to move.

"We go," he said, as they marched toward the door. "Hold firm."

There came a snap, and a fizzle, as if Low Port's spotty power grid had achieved one of its frequent overloads.

Ahead of them, the door sagged on its hinges.

Mar Tyn extended a hand and pushed it out of his way.

#

The riot had dissolved into isolated pockets of violence along the street – and what looked to be a full-fledged brawl across from the bakery, and isolated pockets of violence up and down the street.

Mar Tyn's feet walked steadily and with assurance down the littered street, detouring around rocks, and bodies, and other debris. The child in his arms scarcely seemed to breathe.

He had the side door of the bakery in his eye before the shout he had been expecting came from behind. His feet did not falter; he walked, not even looking aside.

"I'll kill you both!" Her Nin bey'Pasra roared. Heavy footsteps thundered from behind.

Ahead, the bakery door burst open. Fireyn had a gun in her hand, and her face was terrible to see. Cisco held the door, also showing a gun, and Don Eyr was scarcely behind him, shouting.

Mar Tyn's feet deigned at last to run. A shot sounded from behind, a second, and a thud, as if a sack of rocks had hit the street. His foot struck a rock, and he stumbled, throwing himself forward, into Don Eyr's arms.

The three of them pulled back into safety of the hallway; Fireyn leaping in behind.

Cisco slammed the door.

"Done?" he asked.

"Done and dead," she answered.

"What happened?" Don Eyr asked nearer at hand. He straightened slowly, one hand on Mar Tyn's shoulder; one hand on Aazali's narrow back.

"I'll tell you everything," Mar Tyn said. "But first – the child."

"Yes," Don Eyr said. "First – the child."

SIX

The streets were recovered from the war; the rubble had been cleared away, the Gossip Roost rebuilt. Repairs had been made as needed. Classes had resumed.

Aazali sen'Pero and Mar Tyn eys'Ornstahl – well-fed, well-washed, well-dressed – stood in the large parlor, with Don Eyr, and Serana, and Fireyn.

"You should have a third," Serana said, not for the first time, "to guard your back."

It was prudent, but Mar Tyn's feet, rebels that they were, would have none of it.

"Myself, and Aazali," he said. "We cannot arrive as an armed delegation. Mid Port wouldn't understand."

Don Eyr stirred, and sighed, and spread his hands, meeting Serana's eyes with a small smile.

"He is correct, my love; accept it."

She sighed, her answering smile wry.

"In fact, I am over-protective."

"We share the fault," Fireyn said. She turned a stern eye on him. "Mar Tyn. You will be *prudent*."

He smiled at her with new-learned tenderness.

"Now, how can I promise that?"

Almost, she smiled in turn. Almost.

"Do what you might, then," she said.

"I will."

Serana dropped to one knee and opened her arms.

"My child, remember us. If you have need, come. You will always have a place with us."

"Thank you," Aazali said, and threw herself into the large embrace. "I might stay here," she whispered, but Serana put her at arm's length and shook her head.

"We cannot train you, and training you *must* have, for your own protection and that of your friends. If, when you are trained, you choose to come back to us, we will have you, gladly."

"Yes," said Aazali. They had, after all, been over this, many times.

She turned, then, to hug Don Eyr, then Fireyn, and at last came back to his side, slipping her small warm hand into his.

"Mar Tyn," she said, looking up into his face with grey eyes still shadowed from all she had endured. "It is time for us to go."

SEVEN

Some hours later, and they were in Mid Port. Thus far, no one had taken notice of them, neatly dressed and cleanly as they were. Mar Tyn was at one with his feet, as they walked into the pretty court, with its flowers and fountains, and the house just there, as if waiting for them.

Aazali's grip on his hand tightened on his as they climbed the stairs.

"Mar Tyn," she said, when they had finished the flight, and stood before the polished wooden door.

"Mar Tyn, what if they don't want me?"

This was not a new question, either, but he did not fault her for asking again.

"They would be fools, not to want you," he said patiently. "If it happens that they *are* fools, we will return to the bakery, and make another plan."

"Yes," she breathed, and he raised his free hand to touch the bell-pad.

Three notes sounded, muted by the door.

They waited.

The door opened, revealing a halfling with wide blue eyes and curling yellow hair. Doubtless, his face was pleasing enough when he smiled. But he was not smiling. He barely glanced at Aazali, his attention was all for Mar Tyn, or, rather, whatever he saw just beyond Mar Tyn's shoulder, which plainly pleased him not at all.

"We want none of your sort here," he said shortly. "Go, before the hall master comes."

It might, Mar Tyn thought, have been kindness, of its sort. He chose to believe so.

"You want none of my sort," he agreed. "But this child is one of yours, Healer, and the Hall holds an obligation to train her."

The boy's frown grew marked.

"Tainted. . ." he began – and spun as a shadow flickered behind him, and a plump woman, her pale red hair pulled into a long tail behind her head, stepped to his side.

"I will take care of these gentles, Tin Non," she said.

"Yes, Healer." The doorkeeper bowed and left them.

Mar Tyn met the Healer's pale blue eyes. She was, he thought, with a small shock, no older than he was. Surely, this was not the hall master.

"Tin Non gives you good advice," she told him. "You should be gone before the hall master arrives. We have perhaps twelve minutes."

With that she turned to the child standing very still beside him, her grip bruising his fingers.

She bent, her eyes on the child – and abruptly went to her knees, as if what she saw there were too much to bear, standing.

"So young," Mar Tyn heard her whisper, before she extended a plump hand.

"My name is Dyoli," she said softly. "May I know yours?"

"Aazali," the child said, ignoring the outstretched hand. "I am Aazali sen'Pero. And this is *my friend*, Mar Tyn eys'Ornstahl."

There was a small pause, during which the Healer slanted her eyes at him, before returning her attention to Aazali.

"I see that he is your good friend," she said, softly. "He is very brave to bring you here, placing himself so much at risk. I see that you honor him. I honor him, too."

She paused, as if she were scrutinizing something visible to only herself.

"We in this Hall will take care of you," she said, after a moment.

"Serana said you would train me," Aazali answered.

Healer Dyoli bowed her head.

"We will do that, also. But first, we will take care of you," she said softly, and offered her hand again. "Will you come with me?"

The child stiffened, her fingers tightening. Mar Tyn dropped to his heels, so that all of their faces were level.

"Aazali, this is what we had talked about," he said gently. "This is the *best* outcome to our plan."

"Yes," she said, then, and of a sudden threw herself around his neck.

"Stay safe," she said, her voice breaking on a sob. "Mar Tyn, *promise* me."

"Child, as safe as I may. You know that is everything I can promise."

"Yes," she said again, and he felt her whole body shudder as she sighed.

She moved her head, and kissed his cheek, then pushed against his shoulder.

He let her go, and watched as she stepped forward and at last took the Healer's hand.

"Thank you," she said, subdued, but willing.

"Thank you, Sister," the Healer answered, rising slowly. "I will do my best to be worthy of you."

Mar Tyn rose, as well, and cleared his throat. She looked to him.

"I have," he said, reaching toward an inner pocket. "Funds for the child's keep. Her mother is dead. She has no clan, no kin."

The Healer frowned, glanced past his shoulder, then looked into his face.

"The Hall will keep her, and I will myself take her under my care. You – use your money to secure your fortune, Mar Tyn eys'Ornstahl. I. . .feel, *very strongly*, that you ought to do so."

He blinked at her, momentarily wordless, but there – it was said that some Healers saw ahead in time.

"Thank you," he said. "I will take your advice."

She glanced behind her suddenly, the long tail of her hair swinging, and stepped back into the hallway, drawing Aazali with her.

"The hall master. Go, quickly! Stay as safe as you are able, Mar Tyn."

The door closed, and he turned, at one with his feet – down the stairs, and out of the courtyard, into the wide street, walking brisk and light, away from Mid Port – back to Low Port and his fortune.

SUREBLEAK

Dudley Avenue and Farley Lane

It might have been thunder that waked Daav.

If so, it waked *only* him. His bedmates slumbered on, Kamele's head on Aelliana's shoulder; a pleasant picture, which he tarried a moment to admire before slipping out from beneath the blankets.

His pants came easily to hand, and he pulled them on before turning toward the window. A line of light showed at the edge of the drawn shade; he eased it up a fraction and gazed upon a street filled with shadows, along which street lights glowed. Above, the sky showed the faintest streaks of peach and cream.

Well, then, possibly it had only thundered in his dreams. It would not have been the first time.

He let the shade fall back, looking again to the bed, and the pair sleeping there. Given the advancing hour, he really ought to wake them. Surely they had tried Kareen's patience – and her hospitality – far enough. He and Aelliana had stopped yesterday for a morning visit, to make themselves known to one who deserved the truth from them, and expecting – on his side – to have been summarily dismissed.

Instead, they had proceeded to monopolize Kamele all day and night, nor had she been an unwilling participant.

In retrospect, it could hardly have been otherwise. After so much time apart, and so many adventures, in which Aelliana's physical presence, and his own abrupt youthening, were not the least strange – of *course* it would take hours – days! – to catch

74

themselves up. It had been his error, to expect that Kamele would meet them coldly. His *grievous* error, unworthy of the man who had been Kamele Waitley's *onagrata* for twenty Standards.

Well, and he had his error shown to him, vigorously, and they three had filled in the broad outlines of their lives since last they'd been together. That, at least. His sister had been forbearing, perhaps even kind – witness the discreet series of trays sent up to the scholar's rooms, and the lack of a call to Prime.

To tell truth, neither he nor Aelliana had planned a bed visit, nor, he was persuaded, had Kamele. Yet, when the moment came, it had been recognized by all, and accepted as inevitable.

So – a touch, and another, a press, a stroke; knowing kisses shared between familiar lovers – and the bed, all three aflame. And after they had rested, once again, comfortable and comforting, before sliding into shared sleep. . .

To wake with a new day barely dawning, and the particular business he and Aelliana had at the port yet to be accomplished. Not that there had been a deadline attached to that business, other than their mutual desire to become properly established as pilots, and certified to fly.

He considered the bed, and the choices before him: To wake them, or not to wake them? Surely, whichever it came to, it would be *them*; he was done with sneaking away from Kamele while she slept.

As he stood contemplating his best course, there came a discreet knock at the door, which was very likely their eviction notice, solving the problem for them all.

Running his hands over his short-cropped hair, he crossed the room and opened the door, expecting to see his sister, properly chilly in her irritation.

Instead, there was another tray on the table beside the door, a multitude of small covered plates clustered on it, with a steaming teapot, and a carafe of morning wine nestled next to a small vase holding three small dark red flowers.

Well.

He picked up the tray, brought it into the room, and put it on the table by the window.

Daav, Aelliana murmured inside his head; *has Kareen had enough of us?*

Very much the contrary, he told her. *True affection is honored, and we are invited to make merry.*

We have *made merry*, Aelliana pointed out.

Ah, but have we been merry thrice? He asked, focusing deliberately on the vase and its contents.

There was a flicker of. . .something from Aelliana. Perhaps it was astonishment.

Kareen *sent that*?

So I suppose, as it was Kareen who urged us to call and make our bows. She must feel a certain proprietary interest. And she does appear genuinely fond of Kamele.

She is. . .much changed, Aelliana offered eventually.

I am told that age mellows, he answered. *Not that I would know, of course.*

Of course, his lifemate said politely. *If you have done fussing with the tray, you might come and help me wake Kamele.*

Daav smiled, and bowed gently to the three bold flowers in their vase.

Certainly, he said. *After all, one would scarcely wish to disoblige one's sister.*

\#

Later, having obliged Kareen most thoroughly, they tardily addressed breakfast, each telling over the tasks of the advancing day.

"We have two ships to inspect, so that we may vigorously debate the merits of each," Aelliana said, sipping the last of her tea.

Kamele tipped her head to one side. Her hair was still damp from the shower, and droplets glittered like gemstones, strung through her pale hair.

"Will you set up as small traders?" she asked.

"As couriers," Aelliana said. "We are quite unsuited to be traders, I fear."

"And it must be said," Daav added, "that the potential of randomized danger draws her, like a moth to flame."

"Very true," Aelliana said gravely. "Besides, you know, if I fail to fall into enough scrapes from which I must be extracted, Daav becomes bored, which I am certain you agree is something to be avoided."

Kamele laughed.

"When he's bored, he takes things apart," she said, giving Aelliana a comradely nod, "as you know. You'd definitely want to avoid that, on a spaceship."

"Unkind!" Daav protested; "I always put them back together again!"

He put his empty cup on the table, met Kamele's eye, and lifted a shoulder in a rueful half-shrug. "Nearly always."

She laughed again.

"Do you plan an immediate lift?"

"Not quite immediately," Aelliana said. "The debating of merits may take some time. Also, we must be tested for new licenses."

Kamele frowned, and glanced to Daav.

"Theo tells me that a master pilot's license never expires."

"Very true, but in the particular case, it is – *more expedient*, let us say – to obtain a new license under a new name than to undertake an explanation of my current estate to either the Pilots Guild or to the Scouts."

"The delm is adamant," Aelliana added. "We must qualify on our current abilities, and the tickets we fly on must be true."

"No falsifying sources," Kamele said wisely, and was rewarded with a wide smile.

"Exactly so."

"And you?" Daav said. "Are you entirely fixed on resigning your position at Delgado?"

"Yes. I'll be sending my letter this week. I expect Admin will be delighted. I've been more of a thorn in their side than a rose in their crown, lately."

"I wonder. . ." Aelliana said, and hesitated, casting Kamele a conscious look. "I fear that I am about to meddle."

Kamele met her eyes blandly.

"Well, I'm certainly not used to *that*."

Aelliana inclined her head gravely.

"Indeed, how could you be? Now that you have been warned, I proceed – Kamele, *must* you resign?"

"What else should I do? Go back to Delgado and be compliant?"

"Oh, no; that would be too dreadful! I was only thinking that – *of course*, you will wish to use your expertise to build Surebleak an educational system. Surebleak, though, is short of funds, and likewise short of scholars trained in the traditional way. How if you allowed Delgado to participate in the project? Would not a satellite school on a planet which is poised to enter the universal conversation increase Admin's *melant'i*, and the whole worth of the university?"

"Especially," Daav murmured; "if they could assign some of their more. . .non-compliant scholars to the project?"

Kamele stared. . .*toward* him, though what she was seeing was her thoughts. It was an expression he knew well.

Our work here is done, van'chela, he said to Aelliana.

We may trust so. And only think what a gaggle of Delgadan scholars might do with Surebleak.

Imagination balks, he assured her.

Bah.

Kamele blinked back to the room.

"I take your point," she said to Aelliana. "This is an opportunity."

"Precisely so," Aelliana said with a smile. She glanced toward the window, now showing a street filled up with the full light of day.

"I fear that we must take leave of you now, to pursue our own opportunity."

She stood, and Daav did.

"Of course," Kamele said, rising with them. "Visit again, when you're able. At least –" She cast a stern eye at Daav. "You might write."

He bowed his head in contrition.

"At the very least," he said softly.

"Now, *that* was effective," Aelliana said approvingly. "I will have to copy your style."

"Be sure to let me know how it turns out," Kamele said. "Now, quickly, another kiss from each of you – and go! We all have opportunity to grasp!"

WHERE DID THESE STORIES COME FROM, YOU ASK?

We're glad you asked.

"Fortune's Favors," arrived, titleless, at the Worst Possible Time – when we were rushing for the finish line on Liaden novel *Accepting the Lance*. Sharon wrote a couple pages, to set up the character, along with a detailed outline, and – sent the story to the back of the line.

Now, there's always the risk, when you tell a story it has to wait its turn, that it will come surly, and go away. That used to bother us, that we would lose a story. On the other hand, we can't write *all* the stories, and we certainly can't write *all* the stories *at the same time.*

So, we've learned to take the risk, and work on the stories in order of importance, and/or deadline. It's a sad truth of the writer's life, for instance, that the demands of a novel will always override the needs of a short story.

So, the nameless story idea, with the new character we really wanted to get to know, was sent to the back of the line, and we hoped it would still want to play with us, after we had finished the novel.

The good news is that the story waited. It had changed a little while it was waiting, but that was expectable, and we were pleased to see the inclusion of a couple of characters we'd worked with previously. We'd been *wondering* what they'd been getting up to!

We also welcomed the opportunity to explore a little more of the geography and people of Low Port, so, in all, we were very glad the story waited for us.

The second piece in this book is an outtake. It was first written to be part of *Neogenesis*, but, as it happened, it didn't fit.

Then, we thought we'd use it in *Accepting the Lance*, but, wouldn't you know? It didn't fit *there*, either.

We're at the point in the novel story line (remember, the demands of a novel override the needs of any particular scene or short story), where this scene can no longer be used.

But! We *like* the scene; we like the banter, and the easiness between the characters, and so, instead of just tossing it into the bit bucket in order that the words could be recycled into a business letter or something – we decided to share the scene with you, our readers, anyway.

You're welcome.

Sharon Lee and Steve Miller
Cat Farm and Confusion Factory
April 2019

ABOUT THE AUTHORS

Maine-based writers Sharon Lee and Steve Miller teamed up in the late 1980s to bring the world the story of Kinzel, an inept wizard with a love of cats, a thirst for justice, and a staff of true power.

Since then, the husband-and-wife team have written dozens of short stories and twenty plus novels, most set in their star-spanning, nationally-bestselling, Liaden Universe®.

Before settling down to the serene and stable life of a science fiction and fantasy writer, Steve was a traveling poet, a rock-band reviewer, reporter, and editor of a string of community newspapers.

Sharon, less adventurous, has been an advertising copywriter, copy editor on night-side news at a small city newspaper, reporter, photographer, and book reviewer.

Both credit their newspaper experiences with teaching them the finer points of collaboration.

Steve and Sharon are jointly the recipients of the E. E. "Doc" Smith Memorial Award for Imaginative Fiction (the Skylark), one of the oldest awards in science fiction. In addition, their work has won the much-coveted Prism Award (*Mouse and Dragon* and *Local Custom*), as well as the Hal Clement Award for Best Young Adult Science Fiction (*Balance of Trade*), and the Year's Best Military and Adventure SF Readers' Choice Award ("Wise Child").

Sharon and Steve passionately believe that reading fiction ought to be fun, and that stories are entertainment.

Steve and Sharon maintain a web presence at: http://korval.com

NOVELS BY SHARON LEE
AND STEVE MILLER

The Liaden Universe®

Fledgling

Saltation

Mouse and Dragon

Ghost Ship

Dragon Ship

Necessity's Child

Trade Secret

Dragon in Exile

Alliance of Equals

The Gathering Edge

Neogenesis

Accepting the Lance

Omnibus Editions

The Dragon Variation

The Agent Gambit

Korval's Game

The Crystal Variation

Story Collections

A Liaden Universe Constellation: Volume 1

A Liaden Universe Constellation: Volume 2
A Liaden Universe Constellation: Volume 3
A Liaden Universe Constellation: Volume 4

NOVELS BY SHARON LEE

The Carousel Trilogy
Carousel Tides
Carousel Sun
Carousel Seas

Jennifer Pierce Maine Mysteries
Barnburner
Gunshy

THANK YOU

Thank you for your support of our work.
   – Sharon Lee and Steve Miller